Dear Parent:
Your child's love of reading starts here!

Every child learns to read in a different way and at his or her own speed. Some go back and forth between reading levels and read favorite books again and again. Others read through each level in order. You can help your young reader improve and become more confident by encouraging his or her own interests and abilities. From books your child reads with you to the first books he or she reads alone, there are I Can Read Books for every stage of reading:

SHARED READING
Basic language, word repetition, and whimsical illustrations, ideal for sharing with your emergent reader

BEGINNING READING
Short sentences, familiar words, and simple concepts for children eager to read on their own

READING WITH HELP
Engaging stories, longer sentences, and language play for developing readers

READING ALONE
Complex plots, challenging vocabulary, and high-interest topics for the independent reader

ADVANCED READING
Short paragraphs, chapters, and exciting themes for the perfect bridge to chapter books

I Can Read Books have introduced children to the joy of reading since 1957. Featuring award-winning authors and illustrators and a fabulous cast of beloved characters, I Can Read Books set the standard for beginning readers.

A lifetime of discovery begins with the magical words "I Can Read!"

Visit www.icanread.com for information
on enriching your child's reading experience.

*In memory of
Marie Weiss,
my grandmother
—J.P.*

*To Udi
—Y.A.*

HarperCollins®, ♣®, and I Can Read Book® are trademarks of HarperCollins Publishers Inc.

Library of Congress Cataloging-in-Publication Data

Prelutsky, Jack.
  It's snowing! it's snowing! : winter poems / by Jack Prelutsky ; pictures by Yossi Abolafia.
    p.   cm. — (An I can read book)
  ISBN-10: 0-06-053715-9 — ISBN-13: 978-0-06-053715-9
  ISBN-10: 0-06-053716-7 (lib. bdg.) — ISBN-13: 978-0-06-053716-6 (lib. bdg.)
  ISBN-10: 0-06-053717-5 (pbk.) — ISBN-13: 978-0-06-053717-3 (pbk.)
    1. Children's poetry, American. 2. Winter—Juvenile poetry. 3. Snow—Juvenile poetry. I. Abolafia, Yossi, ill. II. Title.
III. Series.
PS3566.R36I83 2006   2005002808
811'.54—dc22   CIP
                                                                                                     AC

❖

Originally published by Greenwillow Books,
an imprint of HarperCollins*Publishers*, in 1984.

I Can Read! — READING 3 ALONE

It's Snowing! It's Snowing!

Winter Poems

by Jack Prelutsky

pictures by Yossi Abolafia

HarperCollins*Publishers*

CONTENTS

IT's Snowing!
IT's Snowing!

It's snowing! It's snowing!

Snow carpets the ground,

the air is a silvery blur

that's whiter than paper,

and whiter than milk,

and whiter than polar bear fur.

It's snowing! It's snowing!

It drifts into mounds,

our car's hidden under a hill,

snow covers the rooftops,

embraces the trees,

and blankets my own windowsill.

It's snowing! It's snowing!

I run like a hound,

I romp and I roll like a fool.

It's snowing! It's snowing!

And if my luck holds,

this morning they'll close down

the school.

One Last Little Leaf

There's a leaf clinging fast to
   a branch,
though withered, it somehow
   holds on,
and a single bird singing its song,
though all of its kindred have gone.

And as long as that little leaf stays,
and as long as that stubborn
   bird sings,
then autumn remains in the world,
and winter must wait in the wings.

December Days Are Short

December days are short, and so
there's not much time to play,
the fun has hardly started
when the sun has gone away.

Today, right after breakfast,
while the sky was growing light,
I ran to meet my friends outside
and have a snowball fight.

We began to build a fortress
then raced our wooden sleds,
we belly-whopped and spun like tops
and tumbled on our heads.

We stopped for lunch, then
　　once again
threw snowballs for a while,
we made a giant snowman
with a really silly smile.

We fed some hungry pigeons
and went sliding on the ice,
my mother brought some
　　cake for us,
a dog ate half my slice.

We made another snowman
and we finished off our fort,
then suddenly, the sun went down . . .
December days are short.

Shadow Thought

The winter sun stays close to me,
it watches where I go,
and my shadow is the shadow
of a giant on the snow.

Winter Signs

Winter signs are everywhere,
the winter winds are nipping,
winter snow is in my hair,
my winter nose is dripping.

Winter's Come

Winter's come, the trees are bare,

no leaf now whispers to the air,

they've dropped away, and in

their place

are filmy sheets of icy lace.

No songbird sings, they've long
   since fled,
no feathered wings beat overhead,
no cricket's click or buzz of bees
now serenades the silent trees.

The air is sharp and clean and cold,
the grass has turned from green
to gold,
in cozy holes beneath the ground
small creatures sleep and make
no sound.

Upon the frozen earth I lie
and listen to the silent sky,
winter's come, the trees are bare,
no leaf now whispers to the air.

My Mother Took Me Skating

My mother took me skating
and we glided on the ice,
I wasn't very good at it
and stumbled more than twice.

My mother made a figure eight,
and since it seemed like fun,
I tried a little trick myself
and made a figure one.

My Snowman Has a Noble Head

My snowman has a noble head,

he's broader than he's tall,

his ears are tin, his eyes are coal,

he has no neck at all.

Beneath his ragged hat he wears

a wig of tangled wool,

his barrel chest is buttoned up,

his belly's rather full.

My snowman has a handsome face
complete with carrot nose,
his arms are long, his legs are short,
he hasn't any toes.

He wields a broom, he puffs a pipe,
his smile is wide and bright,
"He looks like me!" my father says,
you know . . . he may be right!

I Am Freezing!

I am freezing! I am freezing!

I am absolutely cold,

I am shivering and shaking

like a pudding in a mold.

There are glaciers in my stomach,

there is sleet inside my bones,

I am colder than the contents

of a million ice-cream cones.

I am freezing! I am freezing!

From my bottom to my top,

all my teeth are clacking madly

and I cannot make them stop.

Oh I cannot feel my fingers,

and I cannot feel my toes,

now my cheeks are frozen solid,

and I think I've lost my nose.

I am freezing! I am freezing!

Inside out and outside in,

every bit of me is chilly,

every single inch of skin,

I have icicles inside me

and my lips are turning blue,

and I'm sneezing as I'm freezing,

for I've caught a cold . . .

AHCHOOOOOOOOOOO!

My Sister Would Never Throw Snowballs at Butterflies

My sister would never throw
      snowballs at butterflies,
lately, they've not been around,
and certainly not at a dragon
      or unicorn,
both are infrequently found.

She cannot throw any at fishes

or porpoises,

we are quite far from the sea,

and never, no, never at tigers

or elephants,

she only throws them at me.

My Mother's Got Me Bundled Up

My mother's got me bundled up
in tons of winter clothes,
you could not recognize me
if I did not have a nose.
I'd wear much less, but she'd get mad
if I dared disobey her,
so I stay wrapped from head to toe
in layer after layer.

I am wearing extra sweaters,
I am wearing extra socks,
my galoshes are so heavy
that my ankles seem like rocks.
I am wearing scarves and earmuffs,
I am wearing itchy pants,
my legs feel like they're swarming
with a million tiny ants.

My mittens are enormous
and my coat weighs more than me,
my woolen hat and ski mask
make it difficult to see.
It's hard to move, and when I try
I waddle, then I flop,
I'm the living, breathing model
of a walking clothing shop.

Stuck in The Snow

Stuck in the snow,

dad's pickup truck.

"Sorry, dad,

that's your bad luck."

"Shovel it out!"
he smiled and said.

I guess it's *my*
bad luck instead.

I Do Not Mind You, Winter Wind

I do not mind you, Winter Wind
when you come whirling by,
to tickle me with snowflakes
drifting softly from the sky.

I do not even mind you
when you nibble at my skin,
scrambling over all of me
attempting to get in.

But when you bowl me over
and I land on my behind,
then I must tell you, Winter Wind,
I mind . . . I really mind!

A Snowflake Fell

A snowflake fell into my hand,

a tiny, fragile gem,

a frosty crystal flowerlet

with petals, but no stem.

I wondered at the beauty

of its intricate design,

I breathed, the snowflake vanished,

but for moments, it was mine.

When Snowflakes Are Fluttering

When snowflakes are

fluttering fluttering fluttering

down in the cold winter night,

I watch with surprise,

as they fill up my eyes

with uncountable pinpoints of light.

And when they are

BILLOWING BILLOWING BILLOWING

over the ground in the day,

to cover the street with a glistering sheet,

I delight in their lovely display.

When snowflakes are
shimmering shimmering shimmering
gently on top of my hair,
to give me a crown of soft
powdery down,
I wish they would always be there.

But when I am

SHOVELING SHOVELING SHOVELING

till every bit of me aches,

I truly wish then, that I'd never again

see those little white fluttering flakes.

The Snowman's Lament

My snowman sadly bowed
his head
in March, one sunny day,
and this is what he softly said
before he went away:

"In the middle of December

I was handsome, round,

    and tall,

now I hardly can remember

those December days at all.

Oh my stomach's started

    shrinking,

I am losing all my form,

and I'm thinking as I'm

    shrinking

that I wish it weren't warm.

"I can feel my shoulders
   stooping
as my body's getting thin,
my nose has started
   drooping
and my mouth has lost
   its grin,
I am surely getting
   shorter,
there is little left
   of me,
my head is but a quarter
of the size it used to be.

"I am getting hard of hearing

and my vision's little use,

for my ears are disappearing

and my eyes are coming loose.

Through the icy weeks

  of winter

I stood prouder than a king,

now I'm thinner than

  a splinter,

winter's melting into spring!"